WHAT MACHINES DO
DAILY LIFE

Written by John Allan
Illustrated by Esther Cuadrado

First published in 2022 by Hungry Tomato Ltd
F1, Old Bakery Studios, Blewetts Wharf, Malpas Road, Truro, Cornwall,
TR1 1QH, UK.

A CIP catalog record for this book is available from the British Library.

ISBN 978-1-914087-54-7

Manufactured in the USA

Discover more at
www.hungrytomato.com

CONTENTS

WHAT DO MACHINES DO EVERY DAY?

Machines are everywhere! We use them for all sorts of tasks, from cleaning our streets to heating our homes. Life would be much harder and less fun without them.

EVERY DAY MACHINES

Some machines help us do chores, while others get us where we need to go. Machines can also help us relax and have fun. How many machines do you use every day?

LET'S GET GOING!

Prepare to visit lots of busy machines that you might see in daily life. Take a look at them in action, then turn the page to discover what they do and how they work.

AT HOME

Some machines around the home are used to keep things clean and tidy, while others are just for fun!

BEATLES

AT HOME

Radiators are used to warm up your home when it's cold.

There are different kinds of radiator. This one is full of water, which heats up.

Radiator

A lawn mower is used to cut grass.

Inside, an **engine** spins a blade that cuts through grass as it is pushed along.

Lawn Mower

This is used to clean up dirt and dust from around the home.

Dirt is sucked up through this tube into a bag or container inside the machine.

Vacuum Cleaner

A television, or TV, is a screen for watching movies or shows, or for playing video games on.

You can control what is shown on the TV using a **remote control**.

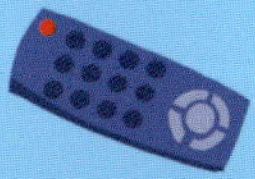

Television

An iron is used to smooth out wrinkles from clothes and other fabrics.

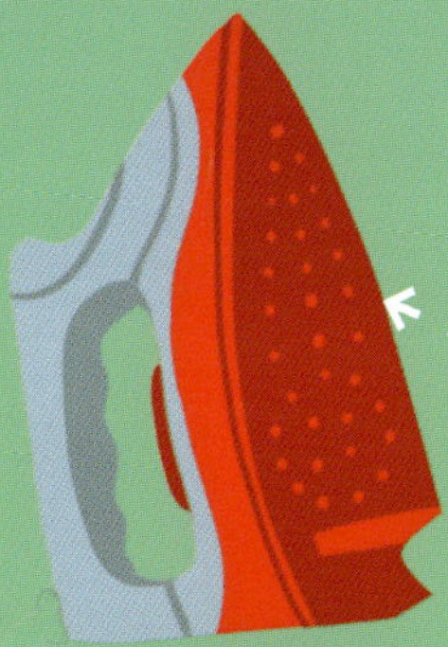

Iron

The metal plate gets very hot and steam comes out of the holes. Never touch it when it's on!

This machine is used to wash your clothes.

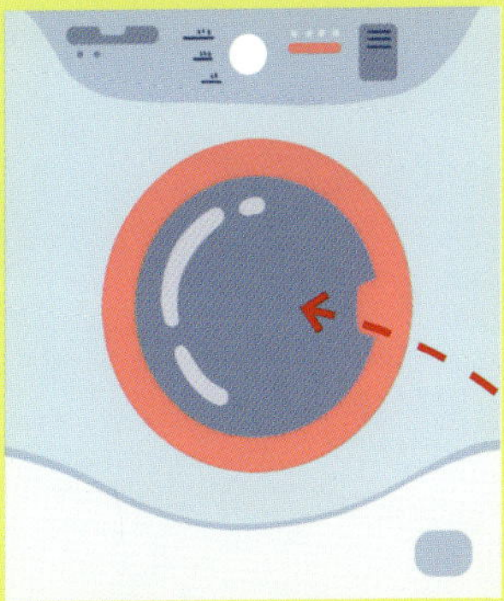

Washing Machine

The hole inside is called a drum. It fills with water and soap, and spins round to clean your clothes.

AT THE HOSPITAL

Hospitals have lots of machines and vehicles to help people who are hurt or sick.

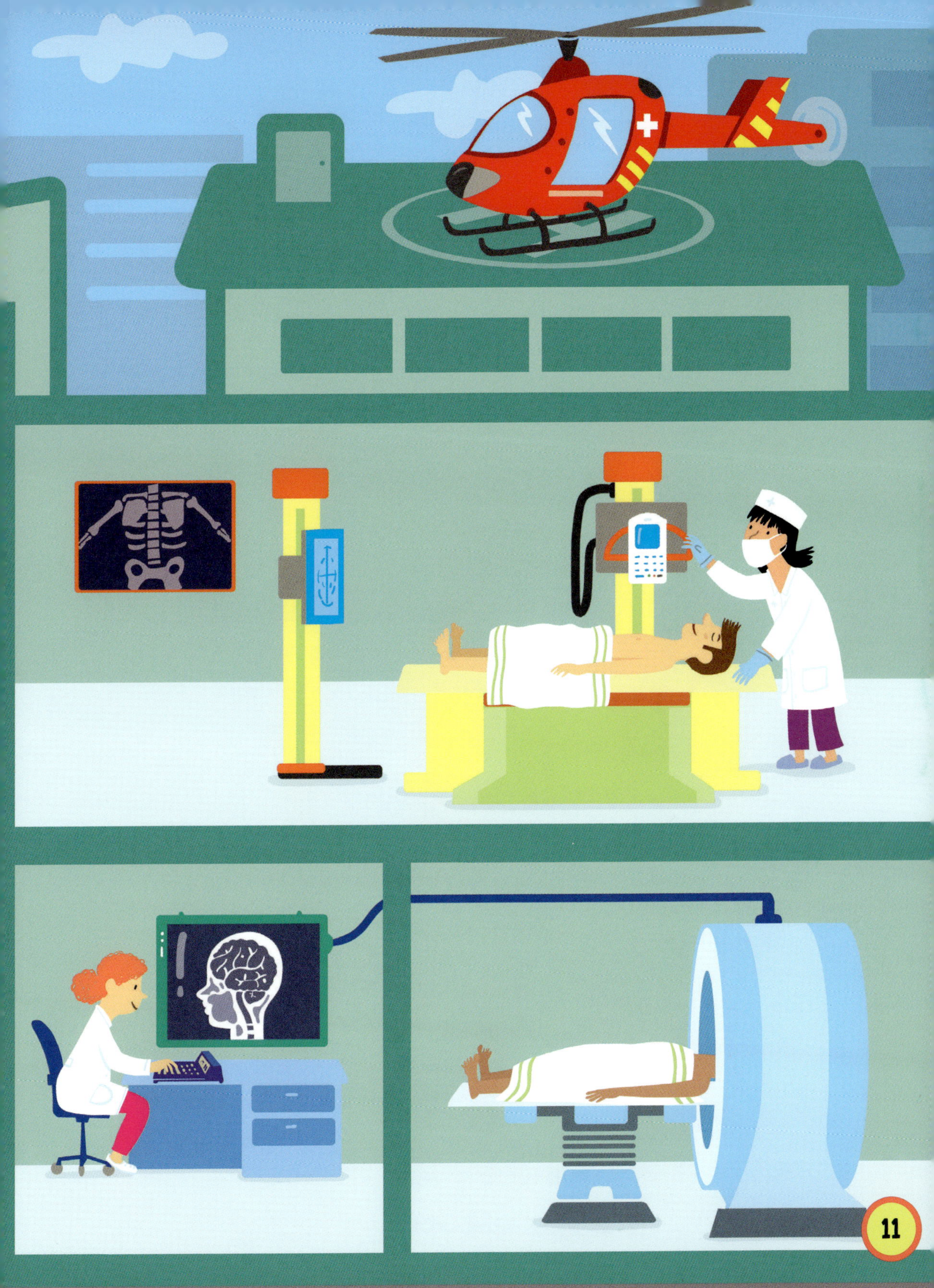

AT THE HOSPITAL

An x-ray machine is used to check for broken bones and other illnesses.

It takes a special black and white picture of the inside of your body.

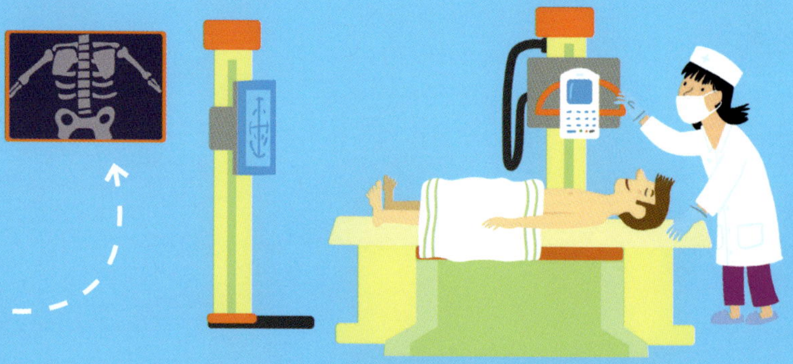

X-Ray Machine

Patients are connected to this machine to keep track of their health.

This screen shows information, like how fast the patient's heart is beating.

Patient Monitor

Doctors use microscopes to hunt for tiny things that can make you sick, like germs.

Its **lenses** make things look much bigger when you look through them.

Microscope

An MRI machine takes more detailed pictures than an x-ray. It can even see inside your brain!

The bed moves inside the donut-shaped machine to scan your body.

MRI Machine

These vehicles take sick people to hospital in an emergency.

Inside the back there's lots of equipment to help keep people alive.

Ambulance

This speedy helicopter is used for emergencies that are too difficult to get to in a regular ambulance.

These blades spin round really fast to lift the helicopter into the air.

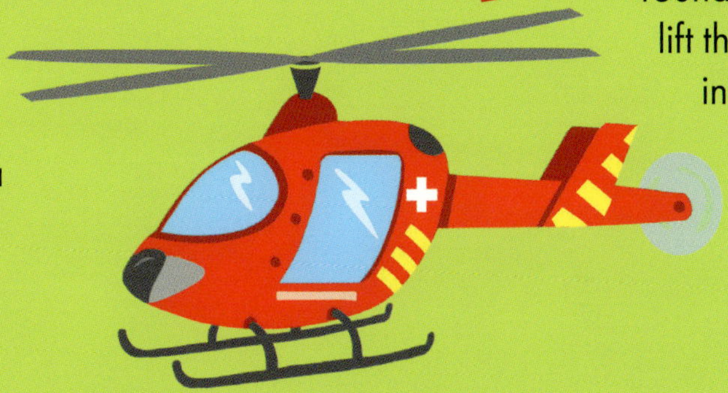

Air Ambulance

ON THE STREET

The more you look around you on the street, the more machines you'll see!

ON THE STREET

These trucks rush firefighters to a fire and help them put it out.

Water sprays out of this hose to put out a fire.

Fire Engine

These lights tell **pedestrians** whether to stop or go at a street crossing.

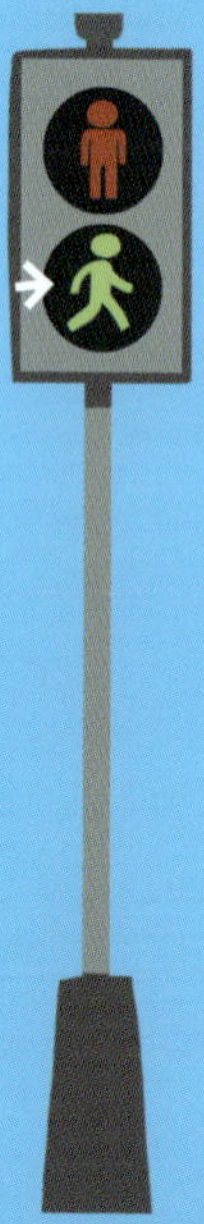

When the walking person is lit up, it's safe to cross the road.

Pedestrian Signal

These machines are often found in walls on the street. It is like a mini **bank**.

ATM Cash Machine

You can use it to take out cash from your bank account. The money comes out from this slot.

Bicycles are a fun way to travel and get some exercise.

Bicycle

Peddles powered by your feet make the wheels turn.

Street sweepers keep our roads and streets clean.

Brushes at the front spin round, sweeping up trash and leaves.

Street Sweeper

This vehicle collects trash from our homes and towns.

The back has a special crusher to squish down trash that is thrown into it.

Garbage Truck

AT THE GROCERY STORE

There are lots of machines at work in the grocery store. Some are keeping food fresh, while others help you shop.

AT THE GROCERY STORE

Freezers are very cold inside! Frozen foods can stay fresh much longer than food in a fridge.

They keep some frozen foods, like ice cream, from melting.

Freezer

A floor polisher is pushed around to keep the floor in the store clean and shiny.

The brush on the bottom spins to collect dirt and polish the floor.

Floor Polisher

You put fruit and vegetables on these scales to find out how much they cost.

Produce Scales

It prints a label so the **cashier** will know how much you need to pay.

A cash register scans the items you're buying and tells you and the cashier how much you need to pay.

This little box can print you a **receipt** once you've paid.

Cash Register

This counter is used to display foods like cooked meats and cheeses, and keep them fresh and cool.

The glass case lets customers see the food, while keeping it clean.

Deli counter

You put the things you are ready to purchase on this machine.

The top is a **conveyor belt** that carries your items towards the cashier.

Checkout conveyor

FIND AND SEEK!

Can you find which machine each of these pictures are a part of?

1.

CLUE: You put things you are ready to purchase on this machine.

2.

CLUE: This machine has a hose to put out fires.

3.

CLUE: This machine can see inside your brain!

4.

CLUE: This machine is used to clean up dirt and dust from around the home.

5.

CLUE: This machine is used for emergencies that are difficult to get to.

6.

CLUE: Peddles powered by your feet make the wheels on this machine turn.

7.

CLUE: You put produce on this to find out how much it will cost.

8.

CLUE: You can control this machine using a remote control.

DID YOU FIND THEM ALL?

Answers can be found on page 24.

GLOSSARY

Bank
A business where people store their money.

Cashier
A person whose job it is to take money for purchases at a store.

Conveyor belt
A moving surface used to transport objects from one place to another.

Engine
Part of a machine or vehicle that turns fuel into energy to make it move.

Germs
Tiny living things that can cause diseases in plants and animals.

Lenses
Clear curved pieces of glass or plastic that can make things look clearer, bigger or smaller, when looked through.

Patients
People being looked after in hospital.

Pedestrians
A person who travels by foot, walking or running.

Receipt
A piece of paper with information about a purchase you have made.

Remote control
A handheld machine used to operate another machine, such as a television or sound system.

FIND AND SEEK ANSWERS

ANSWERS: 1. Checkout Conveyor, 2. Fire Engine, 3. MRI Machine, 4. Vacuum Cleaner, 5. Air Ambulance, 6. Bicycle, 7. Produce Scales, 8. Television.